THE MYSTERY IN THE SNOW

By
Pamela Hillan & Penelope Dyan

Bellissima Publishing, LLC
Jamul, California
www.bellissimapublishing.com

Copyright © 2021 by Bellissima Publishing, LLC

Cover Image Moonzigg by Pixabay

All rights reserved. No part of this book may be reproduced or transmitted in any form or by any means, electronic or mechanical, including any photocopying, or recording, or by any information or storage retrieval system, without permission from the publisher and author.

ISBN 978-1-61477-553-9
First Edition

"Always live your life to the fullest!"

About The Authors & The Book

Pamela Hillan and Penelope Dyan, lifelong friends who used to like to pretend they were in a Nancy Drew book when they were kids, are back again, all grown up (and then some); and they are still pretending! And this is exactly why the Jan and Jenny books continue to be written and why they began!

Penelope Dyan became a teacher, a published writer, a vocalist, and a mother and an attorney, while Pamela Hillan became a mother and a court reporter . . . and then finally, everything went back to what it was before all of that happened; and the Jan and Jenny books were born, beginning with their very first book in this series, "The Mystery On Burgundy Street'.

It was their combined lifelong experiences, and their great desire to do good in this world, along with their love for the law, and their deep concern for humanity, that led to the creation of this latest book in the Jan and Jenny Mystery Series.

This is the sixteenth book in this series; and Jan and Jenny are out to save the world once again, as they begin a new adventure in a cabin in the mountains near their homes, up in the snow. Jenny's Aunt Vi is there, as well as Jan's and Jenny's families; and two new characters, Josh and Sal, come to their assistance!

Take part in the excitement, as you travel through the pages of 'The Mystery In The Snow'; and find out what Jan and Jenny experienced, what they learned, and why what they did and what they learned was so important.

THE MYSTERY IN THE SNOW

By
Pamela Hillan & Penelope Dyan

The Mystery In The Snow

CHAPTER ONE

A CHRISTMAS BREAK

It was that time of year and both Jan and Jenny were looking forward to their Christmas break from school. They both expected it to be a sit back and just relax with a good book time. Maybe they would hop on the bus and head for the local movie theater. All they knew was that it had been a busy year, and they both felt a good, long rest was in order. However, things never seemed to turn out that way for Jan and Jenny.

Jenny's cell phone rang. It was Jan.

"Hey, how about if you meet me halfway down the hill and I'll treat you to a cherry coke at the drugstore?" Jan asked, as Jenny pressed the answer button on her phone.

"Add some french fries, and you've got a deal," Jenny told Jan, jokingly.

The Mystery In The Snow

"Sure thing! I've got money to burn," Jan told Jenny. "And besides, we need to celebrate!"

"Celebrate what?" Jenny asked.

"I'm looking forward to time to relax with nothing to do!" Jan exclaimed, incredulous at the apparent laxness of Jenny toward the revelation.

"Oh yeah . . . that . . ." Jenny said with hesitation. "Well, we shall see," she added. "Have you ever stopped to think about the fact we never seem to get to relax, Jan?"

"Well, when you're busy saving the world, like we are, one adventure at a time, I guess that precludes relaxation sometimes," Jan scoffed with a laugh. "I'm leaving now," Jan then added. "So, get your feet walking!"

"Okay . . .okay . . ." Jenny told Jan as they both hung up their phones. "I'm on my way!"

Just as Jenny headed for the door, her father drove up the driveway.

"Hey, Dad!" she said as she exited the front door and he got out of the car, grabbing his trumpet case.

"What's a 'hey dad'?" Jenny's dad asked with a smile.

It was a kind of a joke between the two of them, because Jenny's dad wanted her to be language specific and to say what she meant and to mean what she said.

Jenny laughed.

The Mystery In The Snow

"And where do you think you're going?" Jenny's dad asked.

"I'm meeting Jan half-way down the hill, and she's treating me to a cherry coke and some fries," Jenny told him.

Jenny's dad reached for his wallet, momentarily setting his trumpet case on the ground.

"Here's some extra money," Jenny's dad told her. "Buy yourselves a couple of cheeseburgers while you are at it."

"Oh wow! Thanks!" Jenny told him.

"And where are your brother and sister?" Jenny's dad asked as he handed her the money.

John is laying in front of the TV watching some old western, and Chris is up the street playing with her friends.

"And your mom?"

"Oh, she and Auntie Vi went grocery shopping."

"And did you leave a note saying where you were off to . . .?" Jenny's dad asked.

"I forgot," Jenny said sheepishly. "But I am telling you now," she quickly added.

"Well, all right," Jenny's dad told her. "I'll accept that explanation for now. But bring Jan back with you and see if she can stay for dinner. I have a surprise for everyone."

"Including Jan?" Jenny asked.

"Including Jan," Jenny's dad replied.

"Can you tell me now?"

The Mystery In The Snow

"Now, you just wait! And you better get going now if you expect to meet Jan at your usual halfway point."

"Okay! Okay!" Jenny told him as she stuffed the money her dad had given her into her pocket and headed down the driveway.

"I can't wait to hear about the surprise," Jenny thought to herself. "I just love surprises!"

The Mystery In The Snow

CHAPTER TWO

LUNCH ON DAD

Jenny started what she hoped was a short walk down the hill towards Jan's house because she really wasn't in the mood for a long walk back up the hill. Luckily for Jenny, Jan had been doing a power walk up the hill to meet Jenny; and she could already see Jan almost catching up to her. That was a big relief!

Jan was waving at Jenny as she continued her march up the steep hill. It was close to a mile between their two houses, and poor Jan had the harder job of walking up the hill, while Jenny just had to walk downhill . . . until Jenny got down to where Jan was . . . and then Jenny had to turn around and they both had to walk the half mile up the hill.

Finally, Jan met up with Jenny.

"It looks like I did most of the walking up the hill this time!" Jan said, out of breath and panting a bit from the power walk.

The Mystery In The Snow

Jenny, with a little smirk on her face, replied, "Yes, you did! And I think that effort deserves a reward, so I'm buying us cheeseburgers at the drugstore soda fountain, compliments of my wonderful father!"

"That sounds great!" Jan exclaimed. "I've worked up a good appetite after that walk! I'll buy the drinks and the fries, and you buy the burgers!"

"That's a deal!" Jenny replied excitedly. "And then we have a surprise waiting back at the house, also compliments of my dad!"

"Really?" Jan asked. "You know I love surprises! Tell me what it is! I can't stand the suspense!"

"I wish I knew!" Jenny told her. "My dad said he'd tell us after we have lunch, and when everyone is together back at the house. So . . . I guess we will just have to wait and be patient," Jenny sighed, to Jan's disappointment. "You know my dad! There's no budging him when it comes to revealing a surprise! It's always according to his own schedule."

That said, the two girls continued to walk back up the hill and over to the shopping center where they were going to have their cherry cokes, cheeseburgers, and fries, all the while contemplating what the surprise might be. And . . . because Jan and Jenny were so excited about what surprise Jenny's dad was going to surprise them with, once they sat down and ordered their food and it was served, they practically

The Mystery In The Snow

inhaled their lunches just so they could rush back to Jenny's house and find out once and for all what the big surprise was going to be.

And so . . . once the bill was paid, they jumped down from the drugstore counter where they'd been sitting . . . and they rushed back to Jenny's house, walking as fast as they could! And the two girls literally stormed into the front door, calling to Jenny's dad, hardly able to contain themselves any longer, because they just had to find out what the surprise was! But where was everybody? No one was answering them. No one was even home.

CHAPTER THREE

WHERE IS EVERYONE?

Jenny scratched her head. Sure, they had eaten quickly, but her mother and her Aunt Vi should have gotten back from their grocery shopping by now.

"This is weird," Jenny mumbled. "Where did everyone go?"

"I have no idea," Jan told her. "But then why would I? It's your family, not mine."

"I guess this means it's a hurry up and wait time," Jenny said, grinning, and then shrugging her shoulders.

And so, Jan and Jenny went into the room Jenny shared with Aunt Vi and turned on the flatscreen TV.

"We may as well have some entertainment as we wait," Jenny said, as she plopped down on the twin bed next to Jenny's Aunt Vi's bed where Jan had taken her place.

The Mystery In The Snow

What seemed like an eternity to the two girls was really no more than twenty minutes, and as they sat and watched a repeat show of 'Murder She Wrote', the girls heard Jenny's family coming through the front door.

Jenny's little sister, Christine, came bounding into the room and exclaimed, "I know a secret! I know a secret!"

"Tell us your secret," Jenny said.

"You have to go into the kitchen and have some ice-cream sundaes with us, and dad will tell you."

"Why don't you tell us?" Jenny asked.

"I would, but it's a secret!" Christine told the two of them. "And dad says only he can tell you the secret, because he's the keeper of the secret!"

"All right . . . all right . . . " a somewhat disgruntled Jenny grumbled as the two girls got up and headed out Jenny's bedroom door toward the kitchen.

It seems no one was home, because while Jan and Jenny were sitting and eating at the drugstore counter, the rest of Jenny's family and her Aunt Vi, were munching down tacos at the local taco stand.

Jenny said nothing as they entered the kitchen behind Christine.

"Are you ready for this?" Jenny's dad asked the girls as he set two hot fudge sundaes complete with cherries and whipped cream on the table and proceeded to make sundaes for everyone else.

The Mystery In The Snow

"Do you mean are we ready for the sundaes, or are we ready for the surprise?" Jenny asked. "Or is this the surprise . . . hot fudge sundaes?"

"Don't be a smart mouth," Jenny's mother told Jenny. "You always have to be a smart mouth."

"Now, now . . . mother . . ." Jenny's dad said. "Jenny is just anxious. That's all."

"I'm being language specific," Jenny said.

"No. You're being a smarty pants!" Christine interjected.

"That will be enough of that," Jenny's dad said calmly as he set sundaes in front of one and all.

"I have a surprise for all of you. And it isn't these sundaes," he said.

"Oh, I thought it was the sundaes," Christine announced.

Jenny shook her head. At least (she figured) everyone was finding out all at once; and she and Jan weren't the last ones to know.

"Well," Jenny's dad began, "I am now going to let the proverbial cat out of the bag, so to speak."

Jan's eyes grew wide.

"I know how much you miss the Christmas snow, mother; and as the song goes, 'It Never (even) Rains In California' . . ." he began, looking at Jenny's mom and her Aunt Vi. "And while I can't get you back to Wisconsin for Christmas, I did finagle a log cabin in the mountains for the week before Christmas! And there is snow in the mountains!"

"Oh, goodie!" Jan exclaimed.

"But how did you manage that?" Jenny's mother asked.

"It was offered to me in exchange for trumpet lessons," Jenny's dad explained. "We will still have Christmas at home, and I'll still have to work and play my horn at night . . . but that's the beauty of where we live . . . from the mountains down to the Hotel Del . . . It's doable."

"I can't wait!" Jenny's mom exclaimed.

"Oh . . . and I already cleared this with your mom and dad," Jenny's dad told Jan . . . and since we'll be driving up to the cabin tonight, she'll be bringing you your suitcase shortly! And the rest of you need to get packing!"

"But what about the band?" Jenny's mom asked, because Jenny's dad never seemed to have a night off from playing his trumpet.

"We'll drive two vehicles up there. You can follow me in the van. And then I'll get back to work. The band can start without me. And I can enter the room with a flourish!"

"It's a good thing I got time off from work!" Jenny's mother said as the doorbell rang.

It was Jan's mom with a suitcase all packed with warm clothes for Jan.

"I hope it's not too cold," Christine whined.

The Mystery In The Snow

"I hope they have cable television up there," Jenny's brother, John, piped in . . . giving his two cents worth.

"We will all have fun!" Jenny's dad announced. "And I wouldn't have it any other way!"

"It will feel like we're home!" Jenny's mother told Jenny's Aunt Vi.

Jenny's Aunt Vi smiled knowingly. She hoped the girls wouldn't get into too much trouble. It seemed trouble just happened to find a way of finding them . . . even when the girls weren't looking for it.

The Mystery In The Snow

CHAPTER FOUR

THE LOG CABIN

The surprise of getting to spend a whole week in a log cabin in the snow was great news, but everything was happening so fast! There wasn't even time for Jan and Jenny to plan anything! And, after all, Jan was all about pre-planning. She liked to be prepared . . . for anything and for everything!

Because the country was still dealing with trying to persuade everyone to get vaccinated for Covid-19, and now because of all of the new variants that kept popping up, the school Christmas vacation schedule had been altered and was extended for an extra week, making the return to school the second week in January, and starting on December 10th! That was almost a whole month off, which pleased Jan and Jenny to no end! More time to do what they did best . . . trying to do their very best to help others any way they could!

The Mystery In The Snow

Everyone at Jenny's house made a group effort to get the family van packed with all of the essentials, and that would be the vehicle Jenny's mom and Aunt Vi would drive up to the cabin, while Jan and Jenny, and her brother and sister, Christine and John, would travel in their second car with Jenny's dad doing the driving to the cabin. It was nearly a two-hour trip, which seemed like a long way to Jenny for her dad to have to drive back and forth to the Hotel Del, in Coronado; but her dad was the ultimate pleaser, and he would do anything he could do for his family to make them happy.

As they were driving up to the mountain log cabin, it started to rain. In fact, the rain came down pretty hard, which caused the ride to last a bit longer than they had expected. As they got closer to their destination, it started to snow.

"Look, Jenny! It's snowing!" Jan exclaimed excitedly.

Watching the snowflakes fall brought a calmness. It looked just like small diamonds falling from the sky, as just a hint of sun peeking through the clouds made the snowflakes glisten. To Jan and Jenny, it was absolutely mesmerizing.

Then Christine blurted out, "Are we there yet?"

She was getting very impatient and totally disinterested in the falling snow. It seemed Christine was all about getting out of the car and having a snowball fight or building a snowman! And she wasn't shy about telling everyone who was within earshot exactly how she felt!

The Mystery In The Snow

"Yes, Christine. In a few more miles we will be there," Jenny's dad calmly told her. "Just be patient. It will be worth it. I promise."

Christine slumped back in the back seat where she was seated, mumbled under her breath, and kicked the front seat with her left foot, unable and unwilling to contain herself, as Jan and Jenny just looked at each other, rolled their eyes, and ignoring the outburst, turned their attention to the beautiful falling snow.

Finally, they were driving through the pines on a long dirt road that (according to Jenny's dad) led right up to the log cabin.

At the end of the road, the car stopped.

"We're here everybody! Let's go check it out!" Jenny's dad happily announced.

And with that, they all piled out of the car, as Jenny's mom pulled up next to them in the van, parking as close as she could to the cabin entrance.

It was time to explore!

CHAPTER FIVE

INSIDE THE CABIN

As the snow fell, the sky turned white, and while it was still rather early, Jenny's mom became worried that it would be dark soon, and that the ride back down the winding mountain road might be dangerous for Jenny's father.

"I'll just take a look around and head back down the hill," Jenny's dad said, reassuring her mother, as he quickly perused the main front room and nearby kitchen of the cabin. "And I promise I'll be careful. This isn't the first time I've had to drive when it was snowing," he added with a grin.

And that caused even Jenny to smile.

"We left Milwaukee the day after I shoveled the car out of the snow," he said, as he headed for the front cabin door to leave. "And that's why we moved to Southern California . . ." he added. "I *never* want to shovel snow again."

"Then why are we here?" Jenny asked, timidly.

"We're here to please your mother," Jenny's father told her. "She misses the snow," he added, as the cabin door shut behind him and he headed for the car.

"I do miss having a white Christmas," Jenny's mother said as she gazed out the window at the falling snow. "But it still isn't home."

Jenny then began to wonder why her mother didn't consider being with them was her home.

"I thought your home was with us," Jenny said to her mother's disapproving look.

"Don't be a smart mouth," her mother told her, with no further explanation.

"Well, let's explore this place!" Jan suddenly announced, lightening up the situation, as she headed for the nearest closet and opened it, peering inside to see what was there. "Hey! There's two snowboards in here!" she exclaimed. "That should be fun!"

"I heard snowboards worked just like surfboards," Jenny added, as her mother just stared at her. "It should be easy for us to do, since we know how to surf!"

"Is it dangerous?" Jenny's mom asked.

"Well, you can't drown falling off a snowboard, so what's the worst thing that could happen?"

"You could break a leg," Jenny's mother quipped.

"I thought that was only said to actors and dancers before they went on stage," Jenny mumbled under her breath, thinking her mother couldn't possibly hear her.

"There you go! You're being a smart mouth again!" her mother told her in all seriousness.

Jenny sighed.

"Let's check out the rest of this place," Jan said, in an attempt to diffuse the situation.

Jenny's Aunt Vi said nothing as John was quick to locate the widescreen TV and discover it had cable.

"This place has everything I need," he said, as he flipped though the channels using the remote.

"I'm hungry!" Christine complained, as her mother opened a bag of groceries she had carried from the van.

"It's a good thing we didn't have time to unpack these at home," Jenny's mother said as she pulled a box of animal cracker cookies from the bag and handed it to Jenny's younger sister.

"Yummy!" was all that was said.

"A 'thank-you' is appropriate," Jenny told her sister, who said nothing as she opened the box of animal cracker cookies and began to eat.

"Did you bring any juice boxes?" Christine asked, as Jenny's mother pulled out a box of juice boxes from the bag of groceries.

"Oh, goodie!" was all that was said.

As all of this was happening, Jan had left the room to explore the log cabin.

"This certainly isn't where Lincoln was raised!" she exclaimed, as Jenny rushed to leave the room and join her.

There were four bedrooms, two with twin beds, one with a double bed, and a master bedroom with an ensuite bath complete with a Jacuzzi tub, and another bathroom in the hall with a shower and tub combination.

"This place is simply amazing!" Jan exclaimed. "Who would have known?"

"My dad is amazing," Jenny told her.

"Your dad is loved," Jan replied.

The Mystery In The Snow

CHAPTER SIX

A WALK TO TOWN

The snow stopped falling and a ray of sunshine appeared in the sky. There was still maybe a couple of hours of daylight left, so Jan and Jenny asked for permission from Jenny's mom to take a walk into the main ski village and to see what was there. It was only a few blocks from the cabin.

"I guess it will be okay. But take your flashlights just in case it gets dark sooner than you think," Jenny's mom told the girls as she and Aunt Vi continued to put away the groceries, making several trips to and from the van to do so.

With a reassuring voice, Jenny replied, "Okay, mom. But don't worry. We promise not to be that long. And we'll help with dinner when we get back. I promise!"

The Mystery In The Snow

Jan and Jenny grabbed their hooded jackets and gloves and put them on for warmth. Then they each grabbed a flashlight, and headed out the door and down the driveway, and straight to the small ski village, which was only a ten-minute walk away, at most.

As the girls were walking by one cute shop after another in the local ski village, they came upon the local post office, which was quite small. On one of the windows there was a bulletin board with several types of notifications pinned to it.

Jan stopped for a moment to read something that caught her eye. There were several missing person notices on the billboard, complete with photographs. This intrigued Jan.

As Jenny walked on to the next shop, gazing at some beautiful handmade jewelry in the window, Jan called out to Jenny.

"Come here and look at this, Jenny! This girl on this missing poster is our age and has been missing from this area for over a year! I wonder what her story is?"

Jenny looked at the picture of the girl. She was a beautiful young teen, with long, red wavy hair, and a beautiful smile.

"Wow!" Jenny exclaimed. "According to the posts on that board, it looks like several kids are missing. What's up with that?"

As they stared at the missing persons that were posted, Jan and Jenny heard a young male voice answer Jenny's question.

"I'll tell you what's up with that, pretty ladies," the stranger standing behind them replied.

The Mystery In The Snow

Jan and Jenny abruptly turned around and saw a very handsome guy smiling back at them.

"Hello there," he said in a very pleasing voice. "My name is Josh. I'm one of the local ski instructors here in the mountains. And you are?" he queried.

The girls at that point didn't know if they should be friendly or not. This guy kind of just snuck up on them unexpectedly, and that made the girls nervous. But . . . on the other hand, they also thought the young man was cute; and he did have a very appealing, as well as pleasing manner about him, once he started talking.

Jan quickly decided it was all right to introduce themselves, so she shyly replied, "I'm Jan, and this is my best friend, Jenny."

Then Jenny, still being curious about the missing person posters, added, "Hi, Josh. I heard you say you knew something about these missing people. What is it you know?"

"Well, for the last few years, some of our local residents have been mysteriously disappearing. There's been a lot of speculation as to why. But no one knows for sure why this has been happening. It's very odd."

Jenny wasn't very satisfied with the answer Josh gave them, but it was getting time to go back to the cabin, so she didn't pursue the conversation any further. She just shrugged her shoulders and tried to appear disinterested.

The Mystery In The Snow

Josh could sense that Jenny wanted to leave, so his parting comment was an invitation.

"Why don't you girls stop by the Ski Chalet Shop tomorrow morning; and I'll treat you to a hot chocolate, a breakfast muffin, or the equivalent and a mini tour of our shop. I'll even throw in a free ski lesson! How does that sound?"

Jan looked at Jenny and nodded her head, and Jenny then agreed to accept the invite. She *did* want to learn to ski, after all.

Then Jenny took a couple steps toward Josh and replied, "That's very generous of you, Josh. Yes! We'd love to see the shop tomorrow. How does 9:00 o'clock sound?"

Josh, happy to hear they'd accepted his invitation, very quickly responded, "That's perfect, ladies! See you tomorrow! Have a pleasant rest of your evening."

And then the handsome young man turned and walked back in the direction of the Ski Chalet Shop.

"Well, good!" Jan exclaimed. "I think it will be fun learning how to ski. It can't be that hard, can it?" she asked, as she looked at Jenny, waiting for Jenny to agree with her.

Jenny, however, was still pondering the answer to that question.

Looking up at the darkening sky, Jenny said, "It looks like it's getting dark . . . and colder! Let's get back to the cabin!"

The Mystery In The Snow

Jan, feeling the chill in the air, agreed with Jenny that it was time to go. So, they both started walking back to the cabin at a quick pace, as the snowflakes came gracefully falling from the sky, landing ever so gently on their cheeks and eyelashes.

When they arrived back at the cabin, it was time for dinner with the family, which the girls helped to prepare as they had promised. After dinner, holding cups of hot chocolate, they sat by a nice, warm and cozy fire and contemplated what the next day's adventure might be.

CHAPTER SEVEN

BY THE WARMTH OF THE FIRE

Jenny laughed, as Jan displayed a whipped cream mustache after taking just the first sip of her hot chocolate.

"Thanks for helping out with the dinner, girls," Jenny's mom told them.

Then she looked to Christine as John grunted, 'yeah, thanks', at them and mumbled something about it being really good.

"Do you have anything to say?" Jenny's mother asked Christine, who shook her head in the negative.

Jenny's Aunt Vi, endeavoring to change the subject, asked the girls how the trip to town went for them.

"It was interesting," Jenny told her. "And it was also kind of scary."

The Mystery In The Snow

"What do you mean when you say it was *kind of scary?*" Jenny's mother asked, after which Jenny told her all about the bulletin board at the post office, and all about the missing residents.

"Oh, my . . . that does sound scary," Jenny's Aunt Vi said, as Jenny proceeded to tell her mother how the handsome young man had invited them to the Ski Chalet Shop where he worked and promised them breakfast and a free ski lesson.

"I hope you didn't say, 'yes'," Jenny's mother told her forebodingly.

"Well . . . uh . . ." Jenny began.

"He was a very nice boy," Jan interjected.

"And he was very well mannered and very polite," Jenny quickly added.

"Still waters run deep," Jenny's mother warned. "You girls can't be too careful, you know."

"How come they get stuff for free?" Christine whined. "I never get to do anything or get anything for free!" she protested.

"I think the girls have a date," Jenny's mother told her. "When you are older, as old as Jan and Jenny are now, young men will want to treat you, too!"

"Oh goodie!" Christine said, as John turned on the widescreen TV using the remote, and Christine ran nearer to her brother to watch along with him.

"I hope there's something good on tonight," she said, for once not even demanding.

"Well, I don't want you girls wandering down there tomorrow all by yourselves," Jenny's mom told them.

"I'll go with them," Jenny's Aunt Vi said. "So, you won't have to worry. But I won't do the ski lesson. I'll wait at a coffee shop or something until they return."

"But you will have breakfast with us, right?" Jenny asked, anxious to have her aunt's opinion of this young man before she and Jan embarked out into the cold light of day with him, a stranger.

"Of course," her Aunt Vi told her. "And I will bet you dollars to donuts there will be a second young man just waiting to meet you two!"

Jan smiled.

"I hope he's as good looking as Josh," she said.

"Josh?" Jenny's mother questioned Jenny. "His name is Josh?"

"Did I forget to tell you that, Mom?"

"You certainly did!"

"Well, at least he was polite enough to tell you his name," Jenny's mother told her. "But don't ever forget that when it comes to things like this, you can never be too careful."

"Things like what?" Jenny asked.

The Mystery In The Snow

"Things like boys," Jenny's mother told her. "Always tell them you want to go where the lights are bright and where everyone can see you!"

And then Jan and Jenny simply laughed.

CHAPTER EIGHT

THE SKI CHALET SHOP

After a good night's sleep, Jan and Jenny were anxious for Josh to treat them to breakfast, and show them the Ski Chalet Shop, as well as hopefully giving them a small tour of the village if he could be persuaded to do so. There were so many quaint shops and restaurants in the vicinity, they were certain this was going to be a great Christmas vacation.

After completing their daily morning routines, the girls grabbed their backpacks, jackets and gloves, and called out for Aunt Vi, hoping she was also ready to go. Aunt Vi was way ahead of them though. She had always been an early riser, and today would be no different.

As Jan and Jenny entered the living room, there was Aunt Vi, eager to get moving.

"I'm ready! How about you?" Aunt Vi asked.

"We're ready, too!" Jenny excitedly exclaimed. "Let's get going!"

"I don't see your snowboards in hand. What's up?" Aunt Vi asked Jenny, as the three of them walked toward the front door.

"We can do that later. Today is all set for a ski lesson," Jenny told her. "I guess you forgot when we told everyone about that last night," Jenny added as they headed out the door to begin the short walk into the village.

Once at the Ski Chalet Shop, they noticed Josh standing by a large window in the shop, watching the ski lifts take skiers up the mountain. The ski lifts were right outside the back door of the Ski Chalet Shop, very conveniently located for skiers taking lessons.

Jenny walked over to Josh and whispered, "We're here, Josh, with my Aunt Vi, to chaperone."

Josh turned around and smiled.

"Hi, Jenny, Hi, Jan. . . and Aunt Vi, is it?" he politely asked, as he extended his hand toward Aunt Vi, to shake her hand.

Jenny's Aunt Vi was quite enamored with Josh at this point.

Then Josh invited them over to an area where a carved wooden table and several chairs to match were decoratively placed next to a floor to ceiling picture window overlooking the ski lifts.

The Mystery In The Snow

"Please make yourselves comfortable, and I'll fetch the breakfast!" Josh said with a big smile. "You can watch the skiers go up in the ski lift, as you look out this window in the meantime."

It was a perfect, almost unobstructed view of the ski lifts taking the skiers up into the mountains from where they had been seated. So that's exactly what they did . . . they watched the skiers go up the hills in the ski lift chairs, two by two, feet bound in skis dangling beneath the chairs.

It was only moments before Josh returned with hot chocolate and some delicious homemade banana bread, which he said was his grandmother's secret recipe.

Josh sat down at the table with Jan, Jenny, and Aunt Vi.

All of a sudden, there was a huge BOOM, and everything in the shop started to rattle and move.

Jan, alarmed, asked, "What was that?"

Jenny and her Aunt Vi looked very concerned.

Josh smiled and replied, "Oh, that? That's just the ski patrol detonating dynamite to keep the unstable snow areas from causing avalanches. It's a widespread practice used for the skiers' safety. You don't want to get caught in an avalanche! Believe me!"

"Wow," Jenny exclaimed. "I hadn't even thought about that! That's a great idea to keep skiers safe."

"Yes, it is, Jenny," Josh continued. "And it's pretty reliable *most* of the time."

The Mystery In The Snow

"*Most* of the time?" Jenny asked, somewhat distressed. "And what about the *other* times?"

Josh sat silently for a moment.

"Uh, the other times? God help you! But if you should ever get caught in one, try to stay calm. If you aren't packed in too deep, you can pat and dig your way out with your hands. It could take a long time, but people *have* survived. It's not *necessarily* a death sentence. The snow will sometimes have air pockets, so you won't suffocate. And you just continue to pat the snow down all around you as you dig, until you get to the surface again. I've lived through it!"

Aunt Vi just sat there with her mouth wide open, thinking of how tragic that would be. Jenny was silent. Jan was having second thoughts about even *trying* to ski at that point.

"Don't worry, ladies." Josh said reassuringly. "You'll be safe with me! And my dad has agreed to man the shop, and I have engaged a friend to assist with the lesson!

"You can count me out," Jenny's Aunt Vi told Josh. "I've done enough skiing in my lifetime already to last me the rest of my life!"

The girls were nervous about the prospect of being trapped in an avalanche, and they hoped that Josh was right that if they were caught in one, they could survive, as they slowly continued to sip on their hot chocolates. Only time would tell.

The Mystery In The Snow

"This banana bread reminds me of Ma's," Jenny's Aunt Vi said, as she tried to ease the tension. "And don't you girls worry about a single thing! I'm sure Josh will take very good care of you . . . *and* if he doesn't, I'm certain Jenny's dad *will* take care of *him*!"

CHAPTER NINE

THE SKI LESSON

Before they knew it the girls were fitted with boots and skis and all that they needed to begin their first ski lesson. Jenny's Aunt Vi observed all of this, because since she was an experienced skier, she wanted to make certain the girls were properly fitted and equipped. The good news was the Ski Chalet Shop both sold *and* rented ski equipment, so there was no initial outlay of money for the individual who was merely interested in giving the skiing experience a try.

Just as Josh finished outfitting the two girls, Jenny said, "I do believe I'd rather ride a horse through the snow . . ."

And with those words, Josh's apparent sidekick instructor, wearing cowboy boots and cowboy hat, walked through the front door of the shop.

The Mystery In The Snow

"I can help with that!" he announced, smiling at Jenny. "I have the perfect little horse for a pretty little thing like you."

Jenny blushed, as Jan looked at her and raised her left eyebrow as if to say, "Oh my . . . just who do we have here?"

Josh quickly introduced his friend as Sal, the Italian cowboy, whose parents owned and ran the local vinery and wine shop.

Since Jenny's dad was Italian, she knew better than to be immediately charmed by this young man. (After all, she did have male cousins on her dad's side that she knew quite well.) She opted to be polite and avoid the flirtation, as would be expected of any well-bred, good Italian girl, even though she was only half Italian, and her other side was Swedish.

"Ciao!" Jenny told him, but not to his surprise, as Jenny looked Italian.

Jenny looked back at Josh, who opened the side door next to where the girls were being fitted and directed them to step outside.

"Are we going up on the lift?" Jenny asked, as Sal took a place at the counter until Josh's dad arrived.

Jenny's Aunt Vi stayed where she was seated and watched Josh and the girls through the picture window, continuing to slowly sip her hot chocolate.

Outside, Josh appeared quite competent. He explained exactly what the girls needed to know regarding skiing in a very thorough and

The Mystery In The Snow

efficient manner. His experience in these matters was being clearly demonstrated!

First, Josh showed them how to glide and move on the snow, and since it was snowing and there was snow on the ground out in back of the shop, this was an easy first step for the girls.

"Very good," Josh told them as he observed the girls following his directive.

"I think surfing is easier," Jenny mumbled, as Jan smiled up at Josh.

After Josh showed the girls how to move forward and then back and then how to turn the skis to sidestep up a hill, he said, "Now I'll teach you how to get up after you fall!"

"Fall? Are we going to fall?" Jenny asked, as Jan continued to smile up at Josh.

"Just pretend you have fallen by sitting down on the snow," Josh directed, as the girls did as they were told, and as Jenny wondered when Sal was going to join them.

" First, point your skis sideways at cross points to an imaginary hill," Josh directed. Then just place your hands right in front of you and slowly walk your hands toward your skis, in between the bindings of your skis and the ski tips. Then, as you walk your hands to your skis, one hand at a time, push yourself right into a standing position."

"That was easy!" Jan exclaimed." So, what's next?" she asked, as Sal came bounding out the door and walked toward them.

The Mystery In The Snow

"I just hope I don't fall," Jenny chimed into what appeared to only be a two-way communication. "Snow is really cold!"

Josh, ignoring Jenny, continued with his lesson. And after showing the girls how to turn and stop, and after he explained what they needed to know in an emergency (other than in an avalanche) he stopped and looked toward where Sal was standing holding in his two hands everything that he and Josh would need for a ski trip.

"I think it's time to go to the lift," he said.

"Don't worry, we'll do this in small steps, and we won't go all the way to the top of the big mountain on the first try," Josh told the girls, reassuringly. "We'll begin with just the bunny slope."

"Oh, goodie!" Jan exclaimed.

"Now you sound like my little sister," Jenny said, rolling her eyes, not so sure about this whole skiing thing.

But the lesson was free. And it seemed they were in very good hands, so what could possibly happen?

Soon, they would find out . . . *after* they worked their way up to the top of the big mountain, of course (which Jenny decided would probably not be today).

"Do you think we'll make it to the top of the big mountain today?" Jan asked Josh.

"We shall see!" Josh told her. "We shall see! You have a lot to learn before we take *that* step!"

The Mystery In The Snow

Jenny just shook her head. There was something bothering her about skiing down that big mountain. Maybe it was foreboding. Maybe it was the knowing thing. She wondered if Sal had the knowing thing too.

As with all things, both good and bad, only time would tell; and Jan and Jenny knew *that* better than anyone!

The Mystery In The Snow

CHAPTER TEN

THE BUNNY SLOPE

Now that Jan and Jenny had a sort of feel for the skis and how to maneuver a little bit on the snow, the next step was learning to ski down a hill. For beginners, that would be the 'bunny slope', which was a gradual, easy to maneuver hill of packed snow, accessed by sitting on a T-bar and being towed to the top of the hill . . . to the top of the bunny slope, that is.

Just as the girls had observed through the picture window, two people sat on a T-bar chair, one on either side of the 'T' hanging from a lifting line, with a small seat on which each skier would sit. So, Jan sat with Josh; Jenny sat with Sal, and up they went.

At the top of the hill to which the skiers ascended, each skier gradually slid off the seat and skied to the side for the next two behind them to dismount, and so on and so forth, all of which was carefully explained to the girls by the boys as they rose up the ski lift to the bunny slope.

Mission accomplished! All four of them reached the bunny slope hill and were ready to ski down it!

Josh instructed the girls on what to do if they felt they were going too fast down the hill, safety being his number one concern.

"Okay, ladies. Listen up!" Josh began. "I'm going to teach you how to snowplow first. I haven't shown you how to do that yet. This is the beginning skier's way to slow down. It looks funny, but it's very important! So please pay careful attention."

Jenny looked at Jan and cringed.

"I'm not in my comfort zone here, Jan. This is awkward. . . And I'm cold!" she told Jan.

Sal tried to ease Jenny's anxiety.

"It's easy once you get the hang of it. Just try and relax, Jenny." Sal told her. "Feel the crisp air on your face. Look up at the clear blue sky. It's just you and nature together! What a wonderful experience!"

"That's easy for you to say! I'm a city girl!" she told Sal.

But she was up on the hill, and she really had no choice, if she wanted to get back down, but to follow the leader, so to speak.

"Okay. Watch my skis as I snowplow," Josh instructed. "First, you bring your front tips forward and slowly move them closer together, as you push the tails of your skis apart by applying pressure on the skis' inside edges. You see, now I have

The Mystery In The Snow

completely stopped. This is also called 'pizza,' because you are forming a wedge, like a slice of pizza. The closer you point your tips together, the slower you will get."

Jan then tried the maneuver on her own. It worked!

"Come on, Jenny!" she exclaimed. "It's pretty easy. Try it!"

Jenny reluctantly tried the maneuver . . . and succeeded!

Happy with her performance, she exclaimed, "This is pretty cool!"

So, with Josh and Sal continuing to give the girls pointers as they practiced snowplowing, it became much easier for Jan and Jenny to begin to practice the art of skiing. In fact, Jan felt so confident, she wanted to try a bigger hill when she was done with this one. But first she had to convince Jenny.

CHAPTER ELEVEN

GOING DOWN!

As it turned out, Jenny didn't need any convincing, once the four of them had completed the bunny slope run to the bottom of the hill where they had started.

It turned out that the Italian cowboy named Sal had pretty much captured the essence of the feel for skiing when he had told her about the crisp air on her face and being together with nature. It wasn't as great as swimming with dolphins, but it had the same general effect!

And as they skied down that little hill, Jenny . . . all smiles, shouted out an appreciative, "Woo hoo!" to mother nature.

As soon as they reached the bottom of the slope, Jenny, all smiles, asked Josh, "Where do we go now?"

And to that, Jan wide-eyed asked, "Can we go to the top of the big mountain now?"

The Mystery In The Snow

Jenny made no objection. She actually felt like she was ready for that! In fact, she was so exhilarated that she felt as though she could practically do anything! Jenny was even ready for the Swiss Alps! (But that was only in her mind, of course.)

"Well, Jenny?" Sal asked, nodding in Jenny's direction.

"I'm game!" Jenny exclaimed. "Let's do it! How does tomorrow sound?"

To Jan's great surprise, it appeared Jenny had (after all) enjoyed her ski down the bunny slope; but in her heart she *knew* that skiing down the bunny slope was a *very* different experience from skiing down the big mountain.

"How high is the big mountain, anyway?" Jan asked Josh.

"It's plenty big, little lady," Josh told her with a Southern drawl. "It's plenty big!"

"I don't care if it's as big as Mount Kilimanjaro," Jenny said, not having any idea at all how big Mount Kilimanjaro was.

Josh tilted his head to the side and asked Sal, "Well . . . what do you think? Are they ready?"

"I'd say so," Sal told him.

"Does that mean yes?"

"Yes. That means yes. These girls are naturals. I don't think they're afraid of anything!"

And so . . . Josh agreed the girls were ready for the big time, and tomorrow they would go right up to the top of the big mountain.

The Mystery In The Snow

And as the four of them walked back from the ski lift to the Ski Chalet Shop, Jenny whispered to Jan, "Sal has no idea . . . Sal has no idea . . . ."

You see, it was true. Jan and Jenny really weren't *afraid* of anything . . . but they *weren't* foolish, and they *never* knowingly engaged in *any* unnecessary risk. And to them, this was no risk at all. After all, what could possibly happen to them when they were just skiing down a mountain, commiserating with Mother Nature?

They would find out soon enough!

CHAPTER TWELVE

JACUZZI! HERE WE COME!

The ski lesson was amazing, but it was true . . . Jan and Jenny were *exhausted* afterward. It was time to call it a day and to head for the Jacuzzi back at the cabin to soothe their sore muscles. In fact, Jan was so tired, she could hardly muster up another ounce of energy to speak!

"Would you girls and Jenny's Aunt Vi like to join us for a bite to eat?" Josh asked, ever so gentlemanly.

Jenny looked at Jan and waited for Jan to speak.

"That was awesome, guys!" Jan told the boys. "Thank you so much for your much needed expertise and fine skiing instruction. But I do think we've had enough for today. My muscles are really starting to hurt . . . and I think I've used muscles I never knew I had! *And* we *always* have tomorrow, right?"

The Mystery In The Snow

Josh shook his head in agreement.

"I can't wait!" Sal said, smiling at Jenny, as Josh continued to speak.

"That Jacuzzi sounds like a very good idea, Jan. You guys should go home and get rested! And the Jacuzzi will be great for your aching bodies. We'll' see you tomorrow. Just remember though to stay away from Avalanche Valley if you happen to decide to take a lift by yourselves. That's where the most unstable snow is, and it can be dangerous if the ski patrol hasn't stabilized it first."

"Don't you trust us?" Jan asked.

"I might trust Jenny, but I'm not so sure about you, Jan!" Josh replied jokingly. "Just don't do anything we wouldn't do. Okay?"

"Okay," Jan said somewhat reluctantly, because she didn't like the fact that a boy was telling her what to do, or rather what not to do.

Then, as they arrived back at the Ski Chalet Shop, Sal decided he would add *his* proverbial two cents worth.

"Yes siree!" he laughed "You gals be careful now! And don't you go gettin' into any trouble." And then *he* jokingly added, "We sure wouldn't want to have to dig you gals out of some mess you got yourselves into!"

Jenny shook her head.

"I think you're taking the Italian cowboy thing a bit too far," she said as they all laughed. "Don't worry. We'll be *very* careful. You can be sure of that! Careful is my middle name!"

The Mystery In The Snow

Jan shook her head in agreement, as Josh mumbled, "I'm not exactly worried about you, Jenny."

And at that, Jan grimaced.

And then the girls took off their skis and boots and returned their equipment to the ski shop counter. Jenny's Aunt Vi got up from where she had been sitting in front of the picture window and greeted them, and they all said their good-byes, with Jan and Jenny thanking the boys once again, Then they began the walk back to the cabin.

On the walk back, right out of the blue, Jenny said, "It sure was great of your dad to let you use his Visa card for this trip, Jan. Did he give you a set amount you could spend?"

"All he said was to try to keep it under a thousand dollars. He knew we were probably going to try skiing or snowboarding, and he knew that could get pretty pricey! Plus, he wanted me to treat you and your family to a nice dinner out on the town! I think a grand should work for all of that, don't you?"

Jenny thought for a moment.

"Yeah, I think so . . ." Jenny replied. "And besides, I didn't tell you that Sal told me we could have a special first-timers' discount, so that should be more than enough."

"How cool!" Jan exclaimed, as the three of them arrived back at the cabin. "Let's get in that Jacuzzi!"

"Did you forget about something?" Jenny's Aunt Vi asked.

"Forget about what?" Jenny questioned.

"You two still need to eat something. You had a big day, and your mother will insist that you sit down and eat dinner with the family."

"I think Mom and Dad will understand," Jenny told her Aunt Vi. "Mom was quite the athlete in her day!"

"She sure was!" Jenny's Aunt Vi said, agreeing. "I tell you what, let me run interference with your mom and dad; and I'll see what I can do."

Jenny smiled. Her Aunt Vi was very good at running interference, and her dad would have to head back to the Hotel Del, if he hadn't already left.

As it turned out, they did miss seeing Jenny's dad.

"You missed your father," Jenny's mother said as the three of them walked through the front door of the cabin.

"I'm sorry. I didn't realize it was so late," Jenny's Aunt Vi said.

"Well, you could hardly be expected to pull those two girls off a mountain!" Jenny's mother replied. "I don't blame you. And all is okay, girls. I made some sandwiches for you after I realized you were going to miss the family dinner."

"I'm sorry, Mom," Jenny said.

"Just don't make a habit of it," Jenny's mother told her. "Being late for things is not a good habit."

The Mystery In The Snow

"I know. I know," Jenny told her. And then she asked, "Do you mind if Jan and I use the Jacuzzi tub in the master suite?"

"Of course not! Skiing is tiring business! Go fill that tub and soak!"

And so that is exactly what they did, as Jenny's mom got out a sandwich for Jenny's Aunt Vi and poured her a hot cup of coffee.

"Thank goodness for coffee," Jenny's Aunt Vi said with a sigh. "I have certainly had my fill of hot chocolate today!"

After relaxing in the Jacuzzi, the girls were so tired they gratefully welcomed the sandwiches made in advance by Jenny's mom, which they ate, along with a can of cold soda, and some corn chips; and then they went straight to bed.

Before they turned out the lights, Jan turned over in her bed to face Jenny and said, "I was looking at the ski runs on a little map from the shop. I think we should try 'Devil's Bend' by ourselves tomorrow. It looks like it's a gradual downhill run from the map. And the lift is only a short walk from the Ski Chalet Shop. What do you think, Jenny?"

"Isn't that ski run on the top of the big mountain, Jan? It looks like that's on the top of the big mountain."

"Oh . . . I guess it is . . ." Jan replied, deflecting a bit.

Jenny yawned; and with her eyes half closed, she said, "I would ordinarily leave it up to you, Jan. But just by the sound of that

The Mystery In The Snow

name, 'Devil's Bend', I think we should go with the boys, or at least they should follow us when we go down it . . . just to be safe."

"Okay . . . Okay . . . then 'Devil's Bend' ski run it is . . . but with the boys! Good night, Jenny. Sweet dreams!"

Jenny couldn't help but wonder what lay around the bend, around the 'Devil's Bend', that is.

CHAPTER THIRTEEN

THE DEVIL'S BEND!

After a good night's sleep and a hearty breakfast, the girls were ready to hit the slopes . . . in particular, the big mountain and the ski run labeled as 'Devil's Bend'. Jenny's Aunt Vi wouldn't be going with them this time, because she felt the girls would be safe as long as they were with the boys. Jenny's mother wasn't quite so sure the girls should go alone; but when Christine persisted that she needed her Auntie Vi to help her build a snowman, Jenny's mother begrudgingly relented.

Jenny's brother was affixed to the widescreen TV, as was to be expected; and the fixation was no surprise.

"Heaven help us when he discovers computer games," Jenny's mother mumbled as the girls headed for the front door of the cabin.

The Mystery In The Snow

"Bye, Mom!" Jenny shouted, as she and Jan began their way out the door.

"Now, you girls be back in time for dinner!" Jenny's mother shouted back.

The walk back to the Ski Chalet Shop was swift; and before they knew it, the girls were back inside presenting the credit card Jan's dad had given her to the cashier, who quickly phoned and confirmed with the carrier that Jan had permission to use it.

"You don't have to do that," Josh said, as he took the receipt and tore it up, and told the credit card carrier there would be no charge.

Jan looked bewildered.

"It's our treat," Josh said, as Sal (the Italian cowboy) sauntered into the shop from the street out front. "My dad owns this place. He gave the go ahead . . . no holds barred."

"What does that mean?" Jenny asked.

"I'm not sure," Josh told her. "But basically, your rental is free."

"Huh?" Jan questioned. "Really?"

"Don't you know nothing in this life is free?" Jenny quipped.

"In this case," Josh told her, "*this* happens to be free, as long as *we* go with you. So, where are we going?"

"We're going to ski the big mountain, like we discussed doing yesterday," Jenny said. "And I have something to ask you."

"What is that?" Josh asked.

The Mystery In The Snow

"Do you know anything about the ski run that goes down the big mountain that's called 'Devil's Bend'?"

"Well," Sal interjected, "you never really *asked* us about that."

"Okay," Jan then interrupted. "Tell us why the run is called 'Devil's Bend'?"

"I really have no idea," Josh told her.

"Me either," Sal added. "But if I had to guess, I would guess it is because once there was an avalanche there on the run, and five skiers were lost and never found. But don't worry. We'll take very good care of you."

Jenny knew there was no use discussing the matter any further. She decided the avalanche story was probably used as a promo tool, along with the moniker, 'Devil's Bend', just to make this place up here more interesting to tourists. Besides, Jan had made up her mind they would ski that particular ski run, and she felt like she was just lucky to get Jan to agree that the boys would go with them.

"Well," Jan began, "we were *planning* on skiing the 'Devil's Bend' run alone, but you guys can come with us on one condition," she told Josh, much to the surprise of the two boys.

"And that would be?" Josh asked.

"We go down the 'Devil's Bend' ski run first, and you follow us and give us a five-minute head start."

"Well . . . all right . . . but then . . . we have a condition too!"

"And that is?" Jan asked.

"You girls will have dinner with us at the Ole' Malt Shoppe."

Jenny was delighted to hear that! Her mother had often talked about the malt shop she went to in Wisconsin when she was a kid. Jenny wondered if they had an old-fashioned jukebox.

"Do they have a jukebox in there?" Jenny asked.

"They sure do, little lady," the Italian cowboy named Sal said, lifting the brim of his cowboy hat a bit, still playing his cowboy role.

Jenny smiled as Jan said, "Well, we will have to get permission from Jenny's mom first. She was somewhat upset with us for missing family dinner last night."

"I completely understand," Josh told the girls, being ever so much the understanding gentleman. "So, if not tonight, then perhaps another night?"

"And there's a barn dance Friday," Sal added. "Maybe we can take you girls to that?"

Jenny smiled.

"That sounds like fun!" she told Sal.

"It sure does!" Jan added.

"Then we have a deal," Josh said. "Or maybe it's a date?"

"I'd say it sounds like a couple of dates," Jan told Josh. "But for now, we need to get skiing, so . . ."

"So, let's head on over to the lifts," Josh said, as the four of them carried their equipment out the door and headed to the big mountain's lift that would take them to the 'Devil's Bend' run.

The Mystery In The Snow

"Can I ask you one thing?" Sal asked Jenny as they headed toward the lifts.

"Sure," Jenny told him.

"Out of all the ski runs up here, why did you girls choose 'Devil's Bend' to ski down?"

"Jan saw it on a map of the ski runs, and she thought it looked like an easy gentle kind of slope," Jenny said, answering Sal. "But I still had my reservations about it, because of the name."

"And you were right to feel that way, Jenny."

"Why? Is it a dangerous run?" Jenny asked.

"No sport is without peril," Sal told her. "Without peril there would be no excitement. And without excitement there is no fun."

"I guess everything is about choices," Jenny told Sal.

The truth was that Jan and Jenny had no idea what lay ahead of them. Only time would tell them that. And the bigger truth was that time simply had a way of keeping its secrets!

CHAPTER FOURTEEN

THE WILD UNKNOWN!

It was a very chilly morning for skiing. There had been a heavy snowfall the night before, so there was an abundance of fresh powder all over the mountain, not the easiest snow in which to maneuver. They put on their boots and skis and got themselves ready for the ski down 'Devil's Bend'. Then they got in line for the lift.

As the four of them got in the lift line and were waiting to grab the next chair to be lifted into the air by the electric pulley system that would take them to the top of the mountain, Josh and Sal gave the girls as many skiing pointers as possible, so the girls could hopefully make the experience of skiing 'on their own' for the first time as enjoyable as possible!

"Jan, I'll ride up with you; and Jenny and Sal can catch the next chair right behind us. This lift moves pretty fast, so get ready to mount the chair and to hold on tightly."

The Mystery In The Snow

Jan, becoming a little nervous and a bit unsteady on her skis, cautiously said, "Okay. But will you hold onto me?"

As they moved to the front of the line, Josh saw their chair approaching and quickly replied, "Okay! This is it!"

Josh gently guided Jan, taking her by the waist, and they stepped in place in front of the two-person chair as it came up behind them. They sat down in the lift as quickly as they could and were lifted upward, gradually taken up the mountain by the pulley system, getting higher and higher off of the ground, legs dangling in the air with skis attached. Jan felt her heart beating, and it seemed to be beating faster than she had ever felt it beat.

Jenny and Sal were right behind them.

Jan turned her head to look behind her lift chair at Jenny and yelled, "How are you doin' back there, Jenny?"

"This is awesome!" Jenny exclaimed. "I love it!"

It seemed Jenny was not as intimidated by the rise of the lift as Jan was.

"Me too," Jan answered back, a bit untruthfully, but excited to get to the top of the mountain.

After about a six-minute ride, they approached the dismount area.

Josh, in a loud voice, so that Jan and Jenny could hear him, yelled, "Just slide off the chair when we reach the top of the mountain and ski to the right and stop until we get our bearings! The chair won't stop moving! You have to move fast!"

Josh was right. It all happened very quickly, but fortunately there were no mishaps. All four of them were now standing stationary on their skis, away from other skiers who were also now dismounting the ski lift. There was a large map showing all the ski runs on a wooden billboard a few feet away from where they stood.

Josh pointed to the far right and said, "Okay, ladies. There's 'Devil's Bend', straight ahead. Just remember to take it slow and easy. And remember to snowplow if you get going too fast, and you'll be fine."

Jan noticed that a lot of the other skiers were more advanced and were taking what appeared to her to be more difficult trails down the mountain. No one seemed to be on 'Devil's Bend', so she thought that was probably good for her and Jenny. Besides, this way they wouldn't have to worry about running into anyone or getting in anyone's way, if that was possible. They could ski at their own pace.

"We will be close at hand, so don't worry," Josh told the girls. "We'll be just five minutes behind you! Let's see you two do your thing! Get going!" he told the girls with a big smile.

Jan and Jenny slowly approached the beginning of 'Devil's Bend'.

Jan swallowed a big gulp of saliva that had formed in her mouth and whispered, "This looks rather daunting, Jenny."

The Mystery In The Snow

"Well, it's too late now! Isn't it?" Jenny scoffed. "Let's get this thing done!"

"Okay," Jan replied, breathlessly. "Here we go. Try to stay close to me! Okay?"

To which Jenny replied, "You got it!" as the girls slowly started down the mountain, traversing the trail to make it more of a gentle decent. Sal and Josh watched from above and waited the promised five minutes.

"They certainly are independent girls," Sal said.

"I like that in a girl," Josh replied, as the girls continued down the hill at what seemed like a snail's pace.

Suddenly, Jan heard a rumbling noise, and she immediately went into the snowplow position to stop and to wait for Jenny to do the same.

"Did you hear that noise, Jenny?"

"Yes. I think it was thunder, Jan."

"But the skies look clear, so how could it be thunder?" Jan asked.

Jan looked back up the mountain. She didn't see the boys.

All of a sudden, there was a loud cracking sound that reminded Jan of ice breaking. The ground beneath their skis began to rumble!

"Jenny! Something is wrong! What's happening?"

Jan was frantic. She glanced up the mountain and saw a huge wave of snow coming straight at them!

The Mystery In The Snow

Jenny screamed at the top of her lungs.

Jan had never heard such a blood curdling scream!

"Jan, it's an avalanche! What do we do?"

"Quick!" Jan yelled back at Jenny. "Let's try to outrun it! Let's ski over this way . . . out of its path! And hurry!"

The girls frantically tried to ski away from the path of the huge tumbling wave of snow, but they weren't fast enough to ski clear of the downfall. Suddenly . . . they were hit with a huge WHOOSH! And they found themselves buried under the snow! Jenny was close enough to Jan to grab hold of Jan's jacket, thank goodness; and by what seemed like a miracle, they found themselves together in an air pocket that had formed under the snow once the avalanche had stopped!

Shocked and disoriented, they just lay there for a few minutes, breathing shallowly to conserve the air they had left, staring at each other in terror, wondering if anyone had even noticed what had just happened. They knew they had to try to remain calm, and they knew that they needed to start packing down the snow around them with their hands in an effort to reach the surface.

But where were Sal and Josh? They were supposed to be close! It was time to pray!

The Mystery In The Snow

CHAPTER FIFTEEN

THE BIG RESCUE!

Josh had taught them well; but as they patted and tried to dig out from the snow, something was impeding them.

"I think that's an arm!" Jenny exclaimed, as she kept working her way out of the snow.

Then a shoulder appeared . . . and then a head. It appeared to be a teen girl, just about the age of Jan and Jenny.

"Do you think that maybe she was caught in the avalanche?" Jan whispered, attempting to conserve her energy as well as the air supply, and remembering she saw no one skiing behind them, not even the boys.

"I don't think so," Jenny told her, as she uncovered more of the body. "It looks like she has a bullet hole in her forehead."

The Mystery In The Snow

"I think this may just be the missing girl who's picture we saw on the post office bulletin board," Jan said. "But it doesn't look like she's been dead that long."

"Someone must have kidnapped her; and when she tried to escape, whoever kidnapped her decided to kill her," Jenny whispered, as she tired of the digging and uncovering of the body and decided to rest.

"That's an awful thought," Jan told her. "But I think you may be right! As you uncovered more of the face, there was a definite resemblance to the girl we saw on that poster."

"It's so sad. She is so pretty. Why?"

'Why' would be the mystery to solve. What was the 'why'? And where was the where? Is this where all those missing kids were? Were they all kidnapped and taken prisoner by some sort of cult?

"I don't know the why, and I don't know the where," Jan told Jenny. "But I suppose . . . knowing us . . . we will find out."

Both girls paused for a moment. They heard something. They heard Josh calling their names.

"Am I hearing things?" Jenny asked.

"I don't think so," Jan said, as the girls began calling out to the boys.

The good news was that the ranger at the top of the big mountain called emergency services after Josh and Sal informed the ranger that Jan and Jenny had been skiing in the wake of the avalanche.

The Mystery In The Snow

They were given some shovels, and a rescue team was ordered, and Josh and Sal led the way down the hill. Luckily, the girls hadn't gotten far down the hill, and Sal and Josh had actually observed where and when the girls fell. And so, the girls did as they were told to do during their lesson, and they waited.

And back at the cabin, Jenny's family waited for their swift return, having been fully apprised of the situation, and having forwarded the information on to Jan's family who were now making their way up to the cabin in the snow.

"Aren't you glad we didn't do this alone?" Jenny asked.

"I sure am," Jan told her.

"Well . . . I guess this is why this run was called 'Devil's Bend', Jenny mused, trying to keep up their morale with some lightheartedness.

And then the girls saw some light coming through the snow! They were going to be all right! But it was too late for the girl that came down to them in the avalanche.

Then Jenny saw something. The girl was holding a piece of crumpled paper in the fist at the end of the arm Jenny had first uncovered. She took the paper instinctively and stuffed it into her pocket, fearing it could be lost.

Perhaps this piece of crumpled paper was a clue.

.

The Mystery In The Snow

CHAPTER SIXTEEN

SAVED AT LAST!

Knowing they were being rescued was a great relief! Jan didn't like being next to a corpse under a bunch of snow! And for that matter, neither did Jenny.

Jan felt around for her ski poles, hoping they were close to her.

"What in the world are you doing?" Jenny asked her.

"I'm looking for one of the ski poles so I can stick it up through the packed snow, so they'll know exactly where we are, Jenny. It's getting harder and harder to breathe. If they see the pole poking through the snow, they can concentrate on one spot as they look for us."

"Great idea, Jan!" Jenny told her. "You really do work well under stressful conditions!"

The Mystery In The Snow

Jan quickly located a ski pole and shoved it up through the snow, hoping it would reach the surface. And it did!

Josh saw the tip of the ski pole pop up out of the snow.

"There they are! Quick! Let's concentrate the digging here at the tip of the pole!" He told Sal and the rest of the rescue patrol.

And before they knew it, Jan and Jenny were free at last!

The girls were freezing A rescue helicopter had managed to land nearby. The plan was to wait for the girls to be removed from the snow and then treated, if necessary.

Josh and Sal steadied Jan and Jenny so that they could come to a stand. Their skis had released from their boots automatically when they were knocked down, so they were able to just walk, ever so slowly, with help from the boys, over to the helicopter to get checked out. Nothing appeared to be broken. But they were shaking, because they were so cold; and they were understandably upset.

"The girl . . . the girl . . . we need to find out who she is! I think we found the missing girl!" Jenny kept repeating over and over again as she was helped to her feet.

"She's not delirious," Jan told Josh as Josh held Jan by her arm to steady her. "There was the body of a teen girl about our age buried in the snow with us. I think she came down with the avalanche."

"Are you sure?" Josh asked. "We didn't see anyone else skiing between me and Sal and you two girls."

The Mystery In The Snow

"She has a bullet hole in her forehead . . ." Jenny stammered. "We need to make sure we get her out of there before she's lost forever."

"Don't worry," Sal told Jenny reassuringly. "The Ski Patrol will get a handle on that! Let's just get you two safely back down the mountain. We'll ride back in the helicopter. Besides, a storm is coming!"

Jenny sighed with relief as Sal put a warmed blanket that he'd gotten from the rescue team over her shoulders. Josh helped Jan with a warmed blanket as well; and they all went over to where the helicopter was, climbed into it, and were flown back down the mountain. The Ski Patrol remained on site to collect gear, remove the girl's body, and take photographs of the immediate area.

What a day! What a day! Now, it was all about finding out who this girl was and what actually happened to her and why. That meant that Jan and Jenny, expert sleuths, once again were hopefully on their way to solving yet another mystery!

CHAPTER SEVENTEEN

BACK TO THE CABIN!

After being extricated from where the avalanche had trapped them in the avalanche snow, and after being returned to the bottom of the mountain by helicopter, where the girls were met by the local EMT services and checked out for a second time, the girls were given the 'okay' to go back to the cabin.

Jan's family had arrived at the cabin by that time; and even though it was only a short walk to the cabin from where they landed at the bottom of the big mountain, it was determined by the EMTs that the girls needed their rest and should not make the walk back to the cabin due to their recent misadventure. So, Josh offered to drive them back to the cabin; and Sal went along with them.

"That Jacuzzi really sounds good to me right now," Jenny sighed, as they all got into Josh's car and headed for the cabin.

"I don't know about you, Jenny," Jan said, "but I'm *really* hungry!"

"I think I'm just tired," Jenny told her.

Then Josh told the girls they needed to hydrate, and drink plenty of water, adding, "I'm really proud of you two girls. You survived a major event."

"I tried not to think about it that way," Jenny said. "I just decided to pretend nothing was wrong."

"Really?" Sal asked.

"Well, not exactly. I mean I *knew* we were in deep trouble; but at the same time, I *also* knew I needed to think positive thoughts, and that we needed to do what we were taught to do to survive."

"The body in there with you probably didn't help," Sal surmised.

"I didn't really think much about that," Jenny told Sal. "I think I was on automatic pilot, just doing what I knew I needed to do to survive. And besides, I wasn't alone. Jan was with me," Jenny added as Josh's car parked on the street in front of the cabin.

The boys helped the girls out of the backseat of the car, and Jan and Jenny's parents came running out to the car to great them with hugs and kisses.

Jenny usually didn't care for such displays of affection from her parents, but this time she was too tired to care.

The Mystery In The Snow

There was a roaring fire in the fireplace; and hot, homemade vegetable soup was steaming on the cabin's kitchen stove.

"That smells great!" Jan said. "And I'm starving," she added, as both sets of parents lavished well-deserved praise and thanks on the boys!

"You are true heroes!" Jenny's dad told the boys.

Jan's sister, Cindy, and Jenny's brother and sister pulled themselves away from the widescreen TV and came to greet them.

"How cold was it under all that snow?" Cindy asked.

"It was freezing!" Jan told her.

"I'll bet you were really scared!" Christine then said. "I would have been really, really scared if I was in there trapped and everything."

Jenny's Aunt Vi simply smiled, as Jan's parents lavished more well-deserved praise on the boys.

Not too much more was said after that, at least not much of anything of great importance . . . and they all went off to sit at the big table in the kitchen where everyone was served hot soup and fresh homemade bread.

"When I get nervous, I cook," Jenny's mother told the group gathered at the big table.

"It's multo bene," Sal said, as Jenny's dad smiled, happy to have a paisano sitting at the table.

And when the warm brownies came out of the oven, Jan was beside herself!

Jenny was so overwhelmed by everything that she had completely forgotten about the crumpled piece of paper she had pulled from the dead girl's fist and placed in her own jacket pocket. Jenny knew there was a mystery to be solved, but it appeared that would have to wait . . . at least until tomorrow.

The rest of the evening was uneventful. The boys left. Jan and Jenny soaked in the bubbling hot Jacuzzi tub and drank plenty of water and fruit juice before going to their beds and falling fast asleep.

Jan's parents and Jan's sister retreated to their RV for the night, since that was the vehicle they had driven up to the cabin, not knowing how much time the rescue would take.

Jenny's dad went off to work, to play his horn at the Hotel Del Coronado.

Relieved and exhausted, the lights went out in the cabin, and everyone quickly fell asleep, all except Jenny's brother, John . . . of course, who had said little throughout the evening, and who remained affixed to the widescreen TV, laying in front of it under a blanket as the once roaring fire in the stone fireplace turned first to embers and then to ash.

The Mystery In The Snow

CHAPTER EIGHTEEN

THE NOTE

A new day had dawned. The skies were clear blue, only a few clouds in sight. The bright morning sun made the snow glisten like diamonds! Soft, beautiful snowflakes miraculously fell from the few clouds, dancing in the blue sky.

Jan and Jenny arose from a great, much needed sleep, and gazed out the bedroom window at the beautiful scene before them. A small group of deer grazed in the distance on thin blades of green grass that were barely peeking out from under the glistening snow.

Jenny suddenly remembered the crumpled piece of paper she had placed in her jacket pocket; and so, she walked over to the chair where her ski clothes lay rumpled in a heap and retrieved the piece of crumpled paper she had removed from the dead girl's hand and stuffed into her jacket pocket, from her jacket.

The Mystery In The Snow

Jan looked at Jenny holding the piece of paper and asked, "What do you have there?" as she walked over to Jenny to see what it was that Jenny held in her hands and was now so carefully scrutinizing.

"This was in that girl's hand," Jenny told her, as she held up the piece of paper, which was now uncrumpled. "I grabbed it before we were rescued, when we were trapped in the snow; and I forgot all about it until just now."

"Really?" Jan asked excitedly. "What does it say?"

"The ink is all smeared. It's kind of hard to make out," Jenny replied, disappointedly. "It says something about being kidnapped, and a Mr. Brindle. And it looks like it says, 'I'm being drugged'; and it says something else I can't quite make out," Jenny told her, before blurting out excitedly, "Wow! I really think that girl was the girl on the poster we saw!"

Jan could hardly contain herself. This was a great clue!

"Who else could it *possibly* be?" Jan asked, agreeing with Jenny's premise. "We need to find out who and where this Brindle guy is! Let's go tell our parents! We slept kind of late, so they must be having breakfast by now! And then we should call the guys! They can help us. They might even know who this Brindle guy is!"

The girls threw on some clean clothes and ran to the main part of the cabin where they expected everyone would be . . . to let everyone know the news.

The Mystery In The Snow

When they got there . . . everyone was gone.

"Now, where in the world has everyone gone?" Jan asked in bewilderment.

Jenny shook her head and said, "I don't know. I just don't know."

And then the girls looked all over the cabin for them, and they looked in Jan's parent's RV; and then they saw them! They were all right there, including Jenny's brother, John, who practically never stopped watching TV; and they were feeding the deer!

"They must have gone out there when we were getting dressed in such a hurry," Jan said.

Jenny raised her cell phone and took a perfect picture of the perfect scene laid out before them.

In the very least, it appeared this would be an interesting day full of surprises! At least the day was starting out that way!

CHAPTER NINETEEN

THE CALL

As Jenny held her cell phone in her hand, it suddenly rang. To Jenny's great surprise, it was Sal.

"This is Sal," the voice said after her 'hello'.

"I didn't know you had my number," Jenny replied.

"Oh . . . I have your number all right . . ." Sal quipped, to which Jenny laughed, as she put him on speaker.

"We have something to tell you," Sal said.

"I'll bet you do," Jenny replied in a somewhat failed attempt to quip Sal back.

"This is serious," he said.

Jan's eyes grew wider.

"Tell him about the note," Jan whispered, not remembering for a moment they were on speaker phone and that the other end could hear her.

The Mystery In The Snow

"Josh is here. And I have you on speaker," Sal told her. "I assume Jan is there and you have me also on speaker?"

"That's right," Jenny said. "But why are you calling us?"

"I told you I had something to tell you," Sal told her.

"And I have something to tell you!" Jenny replied.

"For goodness' sake, will one of you please say what you have to say?" Jan asked, beginning to get very impatient.

"Yes! Please!" Josh interjected from the other end of what was now a four-way conversation.

"Well," Sal began, "you were completely right, Jenny."

"I was right about what?" Jenny asked.

"You were one hundred percent right about the identity of the body in the avalanche."

"I knew it!" Jan interjected. "I just knew it!"

Jenny's face fell. For her, getting this right wasn't exactly a reason to celebrate. She felt bad for the girl in the snow. And while her family might need closure, maybe this time closure would just signal the end of hope.

And even though it had been Jenny who thought the murdered body in the snow was indeed the missing girl, she asked, "Are you sure? Are you absolutely sure?"

"The coroner confirmed her identity," Sal said softly, realizing Jenny was very upset from the tone in her voice.

Holding back her tears, Jenny said, "She had a note in her hand. I took it and forgot I took it."

"What does it say?" Sal asked.

"I think it says the name of her killer," Jenny said. "We were just getting ready to call you and bring you the note."

"Don't go anywhere," Sal warned. "No news travels faster than news travels in a small town. And this place *is,* for all intents and purposes, a *small* town. We're coming to get you two and the note."

"And then?" Jenny asked.

"And then we'll take you to the sheriff, who happens to be my uncle."

"That's convenient," Jan whispered to Jenny.

"Okay. We'll go outside and tell our folks now. They're feeding the deer at the far side of the property," Jenny told him, as she began walking out the front door, turning to walk to the side of the property where everyone was feeding the deer.

"Aren't they cute?" Cindy called out, which startled the deer.

The deer began to run into the woods.

"The deer don't like you," Christine said, as the girls got closer to them. "Nobody likes you," she added. "It's because you're not very nice."

"Now . . . now . . ." Jenny's dad told her. "You two fight nice now."

The Mystery In The Snow

Jenny just shook her head and ignored her sister. There were more important things to consider at the moment.

The girls told their parents that the boys would be picking them up to take them to the sheriff, who was Sal's uncle, because of the crumpled piece of paper Jenny had found in the tight fist of the murdered girl.

The boys arrived, and Josh honked the car horn from the street. Time was of the essence. Jan and Jenny's parents gave the okay.

"Do what you have to do," Jenny's dad told them.

And then the girls ran to the waiting car, piled in the backseat and were off to the sheriff station, the note written by the dead girl in the snow, safely tucked into Jenny's jacket pocket once again.

The mystery of the girl in the snow would soon be solved. At least the girls hoped it would be. But once again, only time would tell, and time had a way of keeping its secrets.

CHAPTER TWENTY

THE INVESTIGATION BEGINS

Jan's parents were a little upset when the girls drove off in Josh's car, because they wanted to be introduced to the young gentlemen who were going to be taking their daughter and her friend away.

Jenny's parents assured them the boys were reputable, and upon their assurances, Jan's parents were much more at ease about allowing the girls to be accompanied by these boys who were helping to solve this missing girl case.

As they were driving down the main drag toward town, Jan came up with a suggestion.

"Hey, guys. Pull over for a minute." She said.

The Mystery In The Snow

Josh momentarily looked back at Jan, who was sitting next to Jenny in the backseat, and then he pulled over when it was safe to do so.

Then Jan asked, "Why didn't you guys even ask to see this note Jenny told you she found in the fist of the murdered girl? Maybe you know who that guy in the note is. Maybe we could just go and check out the situation first and try to get a better handle on this case!"

Jenny frowned.

"I should have known it wasn't going to be that easy!" Jenny said. "I really think we should let Sal's uncle, the sheriff, take care of this."

Then Sal turned to Jenny and said, "Let me see the note."

Jenny reached into her jacket pocket, pulled out the note . . . and handed it over the back of the front seat to Sal.

After attempting to read the note that was partially unreadable due to the smeared ink, Sal said, "She refers to a Mr. Brindle. There's a Bobby Brindle who lives on the outskirts of town. He used to do janitorial services at the teen center. He lived with his grandparents, but they died a few years back. I heard he spent some time in a mental institution, because he was schizophrenic as well as bipolar. I know he inherited the property. That's the only Brindle family I know about in the area."

Jan's and Jenny's eyes grew wider and wider.

The Mystery In The Snow

Excitedly, Jan exclaimed, "That must be the very same guy! Let's check it out!"

"I don't think so," Josh told her. "He could be dangerous. We need to let the proper authorities deal with this."

"Absolutely," Sal interjected.

"But it would be fun if we did a little sleuthing first," Jan grinned and chuckled, as she checked out Jenny's facial expression, waiting for an answer from the somewhat shocked Jenny.

"Uh, I have to agree with Josh, this time" Jenny sheepishly told Jan. "It's way too dangerous."

"But . . . we could do this on the sly," Sal argued. "I have no idea what this guy is really like. I've only seen him in town on a few occasions. He pretty much keeps to himself!"

"Maybe we can just pay him a little visit," Jenny said. "I don't think we should do anything overt."

"Perfect!" Jan exclaimed. "That would be awesome! Let's go find a killer!"

Josh reluctantly turned the key in the ignition, put the car in gear, and shouted, "Let's get 'er done!"

And then they headed for the outskirts of town where the old Brindle home was.

CHAPTER TWENTY-ONE

A CHANGE OF HEART

They hadn't been driving for very long, when Josh suddenly reconsidered.

"I don't think we should do this alone," he said. "This girl was shot in the head! If this is the guy, then it means he's armed!"

"And he's also crazy," Jenny added. "He may be off his meds and fully insane!"

"I agree," Sal said. "I'm calling my uncle, the sheriff, and see what he has to say."

Josh pulled the car over to the side of the road once again, as Sal took his cell phone from his pocket and began dialing.

Jan took a deep breath. She was disappointed, but she knew this was the right thing to do, even if she didn't want to admit it.

Sal explained everything to his uncle.

The Mystery In The Snow

"I can see where you are by tracing the built-in GPS on your phone," his uncle, the sheriff, told him. "Stay right where you are. We're on the way!"

"Are you angry we didn't go straight to your office?" Sal asked his uncle.

"No. But I am grateful you called and didn't try this on your own, Sal," his uncle told him. "I'm on my way out the door, and I'll notify the troops on the way to you," he added, as he walked to his squad car.

And that was exactly what he did.

Before they knew it, Sal's uncle and five additional squad cars had arrived.

"I'm going to let you guys be the lead car," his uncle told Sal. "For all intents and purposes, you are all officially deputized."

Hearing that made Jan smile. No one had ever deputized her and Jenny before this!

And so, under Sal's able direction they led the way . . . all the way to the old Brindle house!

As they all parked on the dirt road in front of the house, Sal's uncle, the sheriff, got out of his squad car and walked over to the driver's side window of Josh's car motioning for Josh to roll down the window, which Josh did. Sal's uncle told the four of them to stay where they were, and to not exit the car under any circumstances.

The Mystery In The Snow

As he left, and as he motioned for the *regular* sheriff's deputies to exit their vehicles and to head to the old Brindle house, Jan suddenly realized exactly how serious this was.

"This is kind of scary," she said.

"It sure is," Jenny told her.

And then Sal's uncle, the sheriff, knocked on the front door of the old Brindle house, one hand on the gun in his holster. His deputies stood spaced out behind him at the ready.

"This is the sheriff!" he shouted. "Open the door!"

CHAPTER TWENTY-TWO

INSIDE THE HOUSE

Jan and Jenny and the boys did as they were told and sat quietly in the car waiting to see what would happen next, parked slightly away from the old Brindle house, behind some tall bushes, but near enough to both see and hear what was happening.

The old Brindle house was situated on a large piece of property surrounded by tall evergreen trees and shrubbery. The house was in severe disrepair on the outside, and the girls could only wonder what it was like inside the house. Windows were broken. The old roof had missing shingles, and the outside paint was peeling. It appeared to be close to uninhabitable.

Jan grew impatient as she waited for something to happen.

The Mystery In The Snow

"Maybe I can sneak around the back of the house and peek in a window without being noticed," she mused aloud. "Since I'm the smallest, it makes sense."

"Just be patient," Josh told her. "Sal's uncle, the sheriff, is pretty good at this stuff."

Sal's uncle, the sheriff, shouted once again, demanding the closed door be opened.

It was eerily quiet. As the front door of the old Brindle house slowly opened, an unshaven, disheveled looking man with dark hair that hung down to his shoulders appeared.

"What do you want?" the man asked in a voice so loud, the four teens could clearly hear him from where they sat in the car.

Jenny started shaking.

"Are you okay?" Sal asked, as he turned around to see how the girls were doing.

"I think I'm just really cold," Jenny told him.

It was still midday, and the sun shown upon the white snow.

Changing the subject, Josh said, "Did you realize that if the sun had come out when you two were buried in that avalanche the snow could have melted and turned to ice, and you two could have frozen to death?"

Jenny shook her head to say, 'no', appreciative of Sal's attempt to calm her. She was just glad it was over . . . well, maybe not

The Mystery In The Snow

completely over; because they still had the mystery of the murdered girl to solve.

"Help! Please help us!" came a loud, high, screeching cry from the inside of the old Brindle house.

"Shut up!" the disheveled, long-haired man at the door turned and yelled at someone.

But who was it?

"I'm getting you all some food and water, if you will just shut up!" he shouted even louder.

Then he turned to Sal's uncle and asked, "Do you have a warrant?"

"I don't need a warrant if I reasonably believe someone is in imminent danger," Sal's uncle replied. "I have a badge."

The man slammed the door shut .

"That's it!" Sal's uncle yelled to his crew, as he kicked in the front door and stormed into the house.

It was eleven men and eleven guns to one, but Sal's uncle remained calm as he held his gun, now removed from its holster, on the disheveled man with the long, dark hair. He reminded himself that this man had already more than likely shot the girl who was now laying lifeless in the morgue, and that he was indeed extremely dangerous.

"Search the place!" he yelled; and the search began.

Room by room, the sheriff's deputies searched the old Brindle house. Jan and Jenny and the boys could hear the voices of the deputies yelling, "All clear!" as they went through each and every room of the old sprawling house.

"Check the basement!" Sal's uncle ordered, and one of the men immediately opened the door leading down to the basement and cautiously descended the stairwell.

And there they were!

"They're here!" the deputy shouted.

There were six of them down in that cold, damp basement, all malnourished, all dressed in rags, all shivering from the cold. One girl stepped forward.

"You heard me crying out for help," she said, as tears streamed down her face. "Can we finally go home now?"

"Yes," the deputy told her.

"You're under arrest! Turn around and put your hands behind you," Sal's uncle told the disheveled man with the long hair, as he reached into his pocket for his handcuffs.

As the now arrested man turned around, he yelled, "This isn't over yet!"

And he lunged forward toward a nearby desk, opened one of the drawers in the desk, and pulled out a gun.

As he turned around and pointed the gun at Sal's uncle, he said, "I'd rather die!"

And then he put the gun barrel to the right side of his own head, and he pulled the trigger.

The Mystery In The Snow

Sal's uncle acted quickly and grabbed a moth-eaten wool blanket from a chair next to where he was standing, and he quickly covered the man, concealing (the best he could) what had just happened from the girls who were now coming up one at a time through the now open door from the stairs that led to the basement.

"Let's get this body removed," Sal's uncle said calmly. "And let's get these girls processed as quickly as possible, so they can be home for Christmas!" he added.

And in the end, it all came down to a crumpled piece of paper pried from the fist of a very dead girl, by a girl named Jenny who was trapped in an avalanche with her best friend, Jan.

And through no fault of their own, and by God's hand himself, six girls were saved from a fate worse than death. And even though the seventh captive child was forever lost to this earth, she could now smile from the great beyond.

Jan and Jenny and the boys watched as the covered body of the man was taken to the ambulance. Then they watched as the six girls got into the squad cars.

"I'll bet their families will be so happy to see them," Jan said as Sal's uncle, the sheriff, approached Josh's car and once again motioned for Josh to roll down the driver's side window.

"We couldn't have done this without you kids," he told them. "And I will see to it that you four all get official commendations!"

The Mystery In The Snow

The girls smiled, as Jenny reached over the front seat to hand Sal's uncle, the sheriff, the crumpled piece of paper she had pried from the dead girl's fist.

"You'll probably need this for the record," Jenny said, already thinking in terms of the lawyer she was certain she would one day become.

Sal's uncle smiled and said, "Thank-you so much."

"But we didn't do anything," Jan protested.

"Yes, you did do something; and you did it exactly right," Sal's uncle, the sheriff, replied.

"But what did we do?" Jenny asked.

"You let the professionals do their jobs; and you did the right thing," he told her.

The boys said nothing.

And then, after thinking a moment, Sal's uncle, the sheriff, asked, "Do you two happen to be *that* Jan and Jenny?"

And as to *that* question, everyone simply laughed . . . because they just happened to be *that* Jan and Jenny!

And after that, a very Merry Christmas was had by one and all! And Jan and Jenny went to that dance with the boys, and they had burgers and fries at the 'Ole Malt Shoppe!

It was indeed a very, very Merry Christmas!

The Mystery In The Snow

"May each Christmas be merrier than the last!"